Almost Invisible Irene

by Daphne Skinner
illustrated by Jerry Smath

Kane Press, Inc.
New York

To Audrey A. Coleman—J. S.

Acknowledgements: Our thanks to James G. Doherty, General Curator, The Bronx Zoo, New York City, for helping us make this book as accurate as possible.

Book Design/Art Direction: Edward Miller

Library of Congress Cataloging-in-Publication Data

Skinner, Daphne.
  Almost invisible Irene / by Daphne Skinner ; illustrated by Jerry
Smath.— [1st U.S. ed.].
      p. cm. — (Science solves it!)
Summary: After a shy girl named Irene learns about animal camouflage, she tries to avoid being noticed at a party and at school by blending in with her surroundings.
  ISBN 1-57565-129-7 (alk. paper)
  [1. Camouflage (Biology)—Fiction. 2. Bashfulness—Fiction.] I. Smath, Jerry, ill. II. Title.
III. Series.
  PZ7.S6277Al 2003
  [E]—dc21
                                                          2002156049

10 9 8 7 6 5 4 3

First published in the United States of America in 2003 by Kane Press, Inc.
Printed in Hong Kong.

Science Solves It! is a registered trademark of Kane Press, Inc.

www.kanepress.com

Irene was having a bad day.

First, Ms. Morris reminded the class that their oral reports were due next week.

"I'd rather go to the dentist than give an oral report," thought Irene. She was shy.

Then Ms. Morris called on Irene twice, even though Irene didn't raise her hand. Both times, Ms. Morris told her to speak up. Both times, everybody in class stared at her.

"I wish I could disappear," thought Irene.

When Irene came home from school, her
grandparents made a big fuss. "Teenie Reenie!"
said her grandmother, pinching Irene's cheek.
"You're getting so big!"

"You're not so teenie any more!" joked her
grandfather.

Irene didn't like being fussed over.

The next morning in science, Ms. Morris
asked how animals protect themselves.
"Roaring and biting," said Adele.
"Hissing and clawing," said Will.
"Running away," said Patsy.

"Three good answers," said Ms. Morris.
"But how about becoming invisible?"

Irene's head shot up. "How do they do
that?" she asked.

"Camouflage!" said Ms. Morris. "Some animals keep safe by blending into their surroundings." She held up a photo. "Can you see the foxes?"

"Hardly," said Adele.

"Not really!" said Will.

Irene thought she could, but she didn't say anything.

"See how they almost disappear against the snow?" Ms. Morris pointed to the foxes. "Their coloring protects them."

"It protects polar bears and snowshoe hares, and snowy owls, too!" said Gerald.

Some animals change color with the seasons. The snowshoe hare has a white coat in winter to match the snow. When spring comes and the snow melts, the hare's coat turns grayish brown, to match the color of the earth.

"How do you know so much about animal camouflage?" Irene asked Gerald after school.

"I learned about it when I got my chameleon," he said. "Osgood changes color a lot. Sometimes I can hardly see him."

Gerald pulled out some photos of Osgood.
"Wow," said Irene. She went home and read
about animal camouflage until dinnertime.

The chameleon is famous for changing color.
Its skin can go from bright green to brown to
gray very quickly. It is not trying to disguise
itself. Actually, it is reacting to the light, the
temperature, the color of its environment or
its emotions. For example, a scared chameleon
will change color.

That night Patsy called. She was having a
sleepover party for her birthday. "My mom's
even baking a pink birthday cake!" she said.
Pink was Patsy's favorite color. "I can't wait!"

"I can," thought Irene. She always felt shy
at parties.

When she woke up the next morning,
Irene thought about Gerald's chameleon. She
wondered if she could disappear by blending
in with her surroundings. "If Osgood can do
it, why can't I?" she said to herself.

It turned out Irene could. She wore pink
pajamas, pink slippers, and a pink bathrobe to
Patsy's party. She even brought a pink blanket
and a pink pillowcase. She had a very good time.

On Monday Irene decided to try some more animal camouflage. She wore the same bright colors that were in the classroom mural.

Ms. Morris didn't call on her once.

Camouflage protects all kinds of undersea creatures. The octopus changes color to match its surroundings. The carpet shark's bumpy skin looks like coral. The mottled stonefish, the most poisonous fish in the world, looks just like a rock.

On Tuesday Irene dressed in green to
go hiking. She blended right in with the
trees and bushes.

In the woods there are stick caterpillars
that look like twigs, speckled moths that
blend in with tree bark, and butterflies
and lizards that look like leaves. Most
baby woodland birds are kept safe because
they are brown, like the forest floor.

On Wednesday Irene wore the colors of the desert rattlesnake—brown, gray, and white. They also happened to be the colors of the school lunchroom.

Patsy and Adele didn't even see her.

Most desert animals—mice, jackrabbits, and meerkats, for instance—are gray or brown. Desert reptiles, like the horned toad (really a lizard) and the desert rattlesnake are also gray or brown. Some desert butterflies are brightly colored in flight, but match the ground perfectly when they close their wings to rest.

Patsy called that night.

"Did you skip lunch today?" she asked.

"No," said Irene.

"Funny," said Patsy. "I didn't see you." Then she said, "I can't wait to read my science report tomorrow!"

"I can," thought Irene. She was still nervous about talking in front of the whole class.

The next morning Irene dressed in the same clothes she had worn on Monday. Her blue top and tan skirt were a perfect match with the colors in the mural. "I guess I'm ready," she said to herself.

Just before lunch, Ms. Morris called on Irene. She walked to the front of the classroom. Her hands were damp, and her heart was racing. "My report is about animal camouflage," she said. "I wanted to see if I could use it to hide."

Suddenly the class was very quiet.
"They're interested!" thought Irene.
"Did it hide you?" asked Patsy.
Irene nodded.

"Tuesday I went hiking in the woods," she said. "I wore a green hat, a green shirt, and green shorts. I was like a tree frog or a lizard—hard to see against all the green around me."

"Wednesday I tried camouflage at lunchtime," said Irene. "I wore the colors of the cafeteria—white, gray, and tan. They are also the colors of the desert rattlesnake, which hides in the sands and rocks of the desert."

"Did it work?" asked Will.

"Yes!" said Patsy and Adele together.

"The most fun I had was on Monday," said Irene. "I wondered if I could hide right here, in class. So I dressed in the same colors as our mural."

Irene walked to the mural and sat down in front of it.

"What do you think?" she asked.

Everybody stared at her, but she didn't mind at all.

"It works!" yelled Adele.

"Awesome!" shouted Patsy.

Gerald clapped his hands and everybody joined in, including Ms. Morris.

Irene blushed. "Everybody liked my report!" she thought.

Patsy and Gerald walked home from school with Irene.

"I just figured something out," said Patsy. "You wore pink to my birthday party. You were trying to camouflage yourself, weren't you?"

"I was," admitted Irene.

"I didn't know you were shy," said Gerald.

"She hates attention," said Patsy.

Irene smiled. "Actually," she said, "I think I could get used to it."

THINK LIKE A SCIENTIST

Irene thinks like a scientist—and so can you!

Scientists investigate. First they observe and ask questions. Next they make predictions and test them. Then they draw conclusions. After that they communicate or tell what they have found out.

Look Back

On page 11, what does Irene observe in Gerald's photos? On page 13, what does Irene predict? Look at pages 14-19. What four experiments does Irene do to test her prediction? Look at pages 22-27. How does Irene communicate what she found out?

Try This!

Take the Camouflage Challenge!

Your goal is to "hide" things in plain sight. Collect five different objects. The objects should be different colors, patterns, or shapes (for example, a sock, a ball, a mug). Stick a piece of tape on each object so you can identify it later.

Now find a place to put each object so that it is in plain sight but not so easy to see. (Hint: Match the color or pattern of each object to its hiding place.)

Give your friend a list of the objects you have camouflaged. How many did your friend find? How long did it take?